LEVEL 2 READER

*FLASH FORWARD*
FAIRY✷TALES

# THE Snow Queen on Ice

A retelling by Cari Meister

Illustrated by Erica-Jane Waters

**SCHOLASTIC INC.**

For the Cowden Family:
Tabor, Laura, Treyce, and Taya – C.M.


For Nick and Sienna – E.J.W.

Text copyright © 2015 by Cari Meister.
Illustrations copyright © 2015 by Erica-Jane Waters.

ISBN 978-0-545-85981-3

Designed by Maria Mercado

10 9 8 7 6 5 4 3 2 1        15 16 17 18 19/0

Printed in China       68
First printing 2015

**O**nce upon a time, there lived two friends named Kai and Gerda. One day, an evil Snow Queen put Kai under a spell and lured him away to her ice castle, where his heart slowly began to freeze.

Kind and good Gerda searched for her friend, and her pure heart showed her the way. When she found him, Kai was blue-lipped and frozen to the bone. Gerda cried when she saw him. Her warm tears melted Kai's heart and released him from the Snow Queen's icy spell.

But that was then. Flash forward to TODAY...

"Hurry up!" called Kaya. "Come watch me jump!"

As soon as Gerta finished lacing her skates, Kaya pulled her onto the ice.

Gerta took baby steps. She wobbled and fell. Then she looked up at Kaya and grinned. "Let's see what *you* can do!"

Kaya jumped and twirled. She glided and hopped.

"Bravo!" Gerta cheered. "You are getting really good!"

"Thanks," said Kaya. "Maybe someday I can be an Ice Wonder!"

The Ice Wonders in The Snow Queen

STARRING JUSTINE!

The two friends watched the Ice Wonders practice.

"Did you see Justine's spin?" asked Kaya. "It was perfect!"

The rest of the team was not as good.

"No! No!" yelled Justine. "You must hop high like this!"

The girls tried, but Justine rolled her eyes. "If that's as good as you can do," she said, "the show will be a TOTAL disaster! I will look like a fool!"

Justine skated off the ice. She stopped fast. Ice shavings flew into Kaya's face.

Kaya stared at Justine as if under a spell.

Justine sneered. "What are you looking at?"

"Someday," Kaya said, "I hope to be as good as you."

Justine let out a long, cold cackle. "Yeah, right! I am the Snow Queen! No one will ever be as good as me."

Gerta spoke up. "Kaya is really good. Watch."

Justine glared as Kaya hopped and twirled.

*She is almost as good as me!* Justine thought. *I must stop her from getting better.*

*But how? I know! I will keep her so busy that she will never have time to practice!*

"Well," Justine said icily, "if you sharpen my skates and put up my posters, maybe I could give you lessons."

Justine took off her scarf. She wrapped it around Kaya. Then she whispered in her ear.

A strange look settled on Kaya's face.

"I'm leaving," Kaya called to Gerta. "Justine needs help with her costume."

"I thought we were going to get cocoa at Snowbucks," said Gerta.

"This is more important," said Kaya.

Gerta's heart sank.

The next morning, Gerta texted Kaya about their plans for the day.

Kaya didn't show up.

The day after that was Gerta's birthday.

Kaya didn't even call.

"Something is not right," Gerta said.

She put on her boots and went to look for her friend.

Has anyone seen Kaya?" Gerta asked.

"She went with Justine," said Inga.

Inga pointed to fresh tracks in the snow.

The snow was really coming down.

Gerta shivered.

"I have to find her."

Soon Gerta came to Snowbucks.

A lady stood outside.

"The storm is getting worse," she said. "Come in and warm up."

"Thank you," said Gerta, "but just for a minute. I have to keep looking for my friend."

Gerta was just sitting down when a fuzzy purple lump caught her eye.

It was Kaya's mitten!

*She must have just been here!* thought Gerta.

Outside, the snowstorm had gotten worse!

It covered Kaya's tracks.

"What am I going to do now?" said Gerta. "I will never find Kaya."

Arf! Arf!

Gerta looked down.
It was a tiny, furry dog!

His tag said "PAVO."

"Hello, little one," said Gerta. "Have you seen my friend, Kaya? This is her mitten."

Pavo sniffed the mitten. Then he ran around in circles barking.

"Okay," said Gerta. "I'll follow you."

Soon they saw a cold, blue light.

"Justine's cabin!" cried Gerta.

Gerta spotted Kaya. She was washing a fancy snowmobile.

And she was shivering!

"Kaya!" called Gerta.

But Kaya could not hear her.

She was frozen in place.

Gerta rushed to her side. "Where is Justine?"

"Gone," said Kaya. "But she told me if I wash her snowmobile, she might let me join the Ice Wonders."

"But you're freezing," said Gerta.

"I am?" said Kaya in a daze.

Gerta took off Justine's icy scarf.

Kaya looked into her friend's kind eyes, and the spell was broken.

Pavo ran around in circles.

*Arf! Arf!*

"Okay, Pavo," said Gerta. "We're coming!"

"Sorry I was such a bad friend," said Kaya. "Justine had me under her spell."

The Ice Wonders in
The Snow Queen

STARRING JUSTINE!

"It's okay," said Gerta. "I know you really wanted to be part of the ice show."

"We can have our own show!" said Kaya.

So they did. And it was the best show of the year!